Acting Edition

I0591991

Christmas at Home

by Joseph Hayes

ISBN 978-0-573-66219-5

www.concordtheatricals.com
www.concordtheatricals.co.uk

No one shall make any changes in this title(s) for the purpose of production. No part of this book may be reproduced, stored in a retrieval system, scanned, uploaded, or transmitted in any form, by any means, now known or yet to be invented, including mechanical, electronic, digital, photocopying, recording, videotaping, or otherwise, without the prior written permission of the publisher. No one shall share this title(s), or any part of this title(s), through any social media or file hosting websites.

For all inquiries regarding motion picture, television, online/digital and other media rights, please contact Concord Theatricals Corp.

MUSIC AND THIRD-PARTY MATERIALS USE NOTE

Licensees are solely responsible for obtaining formal written permission from copyright owners to use copyrighted music and/or other copyrighted third-party materials (e.g., artworks, logos) in the performance of this play and are strongly cautioned to do so. If no such permission is obtained by the licensee, then the licensee must use only original music and materials that the licensee owns and controls. Licensees are solely responsible and liable for clearances of all third-party copyrighted materials, including without limitation music, and shall indemnify the copyright owners of the play(s) and their licensing agent, Concord Theatricals Corp., against any costs, expenses, losses and liabilities arising from the use of such copyrighted third-party materials by licensees. For music, please contact the appropriate music licensing authority in your territory for the rights to any incidental music.

IMPORTANT BILLING AND CREDIT REQUIREMENTS

If you have obtained performance rights to this title, please refer to your licensing agreement for important billing and credit requirements.

STORY OF THE PLAY

Here is a modern Christmas play requiring no Biblical costumes; it is realistic, human, homey. The people in it are your friends, perhaps even your family. The day before Christmas finds the Burgess family busy with the usual preparations and poignantly aware that this is the first year the members of the family will not be together: son Johnny is working in Chicago and cannot get home, and Grandpa Williams' laughing presence will also be missed as Grandpa has died in the preceding summer. But the Burgesses do not sit around feeling sorry for themselves; they realize how happy and well off they are. In a series of humorous and touching scenes, we see sixteen-year-old Julie falling in love for the first time; eighteen-year-old Emily receiving a proposal of marriage; twelve-year-old Janet learning the real meaning of Christmas. In fact, on this day, we catch the Burgess family in the ebb and flow of life, meeting change, learning, living, laughing. The story is tenderly and sympathetically told, and behind it all is the real Christmas spirit. When Johnny arrives to surprise the family, you will feel what they feel.

CAST OF CHARACTERS

EMILY BURGESS: Eighteen years; a striking looking girl with soft eyes and an appealing wistfulness. Quiet, reserved, graceful.

JULIE BURGESS: Sixteen years; a girl full of vitality and fine spirit; lovely in a brusque way; in high school; quick, eager, young mind.

JANET BURGESS: Just twelve; lively; a delightful mixture of child and adult; still youngishly chubby; quick and ready sympathies and emotions.

JOHNNY BURGESS: A boyish twenty-one; athletic, with eyes that crinkle with life and amusement and a sometimes sad sensitivity.

DOCTOR TOM BURGESS: Just past fifty; the father; a fine doctor of the old-fashioned and real variety; impractical and humanistic.

MRS. MARGARET BURGESS: Not yet forty-five, but looks it in a graceful way; pleasant mixture of practical realist and womanly sentimentalist; wise and lovely; her family is her life.

RALPH WEATHERLY: Seventeen years; not particularly handsome but engaging and typical, with a wide, pleasant smile and a slight uneasiness.

SCENE

A living room.

CHRISTMAS AT HOME

SCENE: *The living room of the* BURGESS *home in any town in America on any Christmas Eve, late afternoon. The room is decorated with holly, wreaths, and various other gay trimmings. A large and brightly decorated Christmas tree is in prominence. Spread about the room are wrappings, ribbons, red cord, odd stacks of packages unopened, Christmas greeting cards; the general disorder is inviting, homey, natural.*

There is a large entrance up Right leading to the hall and outside door and front stairway; beyond the hall, unseen, is the large and more formal front parlor where EMILY *later plays the piano [off]. At Left there is a door to the dining room. Large windows look out on the street in the rear wall. The tree is up Center. A sofa and lamp Left; table against rear wall up Right—with telephone—and a table against Right wall. A large comfortable chair with lamp and footstool Right Center. Odd chairs.*

The windows are frosted and snow lies on the sills.

TIME: *Late afternoon, Christmas Eve.*

AT RISE: MRS. MARGARET BURGESS *is busy in the room. She has silently despaired of getting any order into her life until after the holidays, so her work is confined to putting the finishing touches to the gay decorations. She is not yet forty-five—a graceful and handsome woman who has an abiding fear of looking into a mirror or win-*

*dow and discovering her reflection is a caricature of her
conception of herself. Her family has been her life for
some time now—and a good life, too. At the moment she
is placing two red candles in glass holders and trying to
determine where to place the holders. During the following she continues her activity about the room almost un-
ceasingly. [This activity should not interfere with the
action of the play but should emphasize the busy reality
of the home during the holidays. The inventiveness of the
director and the imaginativeness of the actress playing*
MRS. BURGESS *should supply the stage business—and careful direction is the only way to do it properly.]*

EMILY, *the oldest daughter, just eighteen, enters from
the hall. She is slim, straight, with soft eyes and an appealing wistfulness; reserved and graceful and quiet.*

EMILY. Mother, you're doing too much again.

MRS. BURGESS. That's about all Christmas means to me,
Emily—doing more than I should. I'm always too tired to
enjoy it. [*Places candles on Right table.*]

EMILY. What can I do?

MRS. BURGESS. Nothing.

EMILY. But surely ——

MRS. BURGESS. [*Busy.*] You only make me nervous. [*Returns to tree.*]

EMILY. [*Smiling.*] But, Mother, you say that every year.
You work too hard yourself, but you won't let anyone
help you. I think you enjoy it all more than any of us. Do
you now? [*She smiles.*]

MRS. BURGESS. Hasn't he called yet, Emily?

EMILY. [*Goes Left to sofa; sits.*] Who?

MRS. BURGESS. Whoever you're waiting for, dear.

EMILY. I'm not waiting for anyone at all.

MRS. BURGESS. [*Half in jest.*] Oh! Well then, you can run down to the store ——

EMILY. [*Rises.*] Oh, I can't go anywhere, Mother.

MRS. BURGESS. I see.

EMILY. [*Sits.*] You're teasing me.

MRS. BURGESS. [*Laughs.*] I'm much too tired to tease anyone, Emily. I'll leave that to Julie and your father.

EMILY. [*Joining* MRS. BURGESS *in picking up Christmas cards on the floor.*] They'd better stop teasing Janet. She's twelve now and not as quick to fall for their fool ideas. Besides, it might definitely harm her—psychologically. If ever I have any children ——

MRS. BURGESS. You won't be having any children for a long time, Emily.

EMILY. I'm eighteen, Mother.

MRS. BURGESS. You're a child!—Do you like those candles on that table?

EMILY. They look nice.—You were married when you were eighteen. I'll be nineteen in five months.

[*A door slams in hall.*]

MRS. BURGESS. Emily, are you thinking ——?

[JULIE *enters from the hall, wearing a snow suit. She is sixteen, a brusque and pretty wind-blown girl, full of spirit and boyish vitality.*]

JULIE. Hasn't he called yet, Em? [*Looking through Christmas cards on table Right.*]

EMILY. Who?

JANET. [*Turning to wink at* MRS. BURGESS.] Why, that crazy college boy from Massachusetts.

EMILY. [*Rising.*] Alec? I didn't say he was going to call.

MRS. BURGESS. Massachusetts? Do you mean to tell me a young man is going to telephone you all the way from Massachusetts, Emily?

EMILY. He just said he *might*, he didn't say he would, definitely. I wish everybody wouldn't be so interested in my business. [*To* JULIE, *who is crossing to sofa with a stack of cards.*] —How did you know anyway?

JULIE. Mother, where are my skates? Willow Pond is all frozen over again and everyone's down there. [*To* EMILY.] How did I know? Why, you read me part of the letter in bed last night—remember?

EMILY. [*At Center.*] But not that part.

JULIE. Do you know where they are, Mother—my skates?

[MRS. BURGESS *goes to hall entrance, carrying a small chair from Left with her.*]

EMILY. Not that part, Julie—I didn't read ——

JULIE. Well, I couldn't help seeing over your shoulder, could I, sister?

MRS. BURGESS. Now, girls, it's Christmas Eve and I don't want any of that. [*Sets chair in hall entrance, steps upon it.*]

EMILY. Well, I always thought grown-up people didn't do things like that—reading other people's mail, of all things.

MRS. BURGESS. Julie, I've taught you better than that.

JULIE. All the way from Massachusetts! What some goofy people won't do if they're infatuated.

EMILY. *Infatuated?* I guess we're old enough to know we're not infatuated, infant.

JULIE. [*Scoffingly.*] Oh no! It's love. It's real love— Antony and Cleopatra! [*Catches sight of* MRS. BURGESS *who is now on chair tying a large sprig of mistletoe to the frame above the entrance.*] Mother --—!

MRS. BURGESS. Now, girls, you're just making me nervous with your quibbling.

JULIE. Is that mistletoe, Mother?

MRS. BURGESS. We've had mistletoe hanging here every year since we moved in—before you were born, Julie.

JULIE. Mother, aren't you old-fashioned!

EMILY. I think it's a grand idea.

JULIE. Oh, it was all right when we were kids and Dad used to catch us and kiss us under it—but *now!*

EMILY. Julie, why are you such a tomboy?

JULIE. [*Rising—spilling cards across sofa.*] I don't know, Em. Why is everything the way it is? What makes you write verse?

MRS. BURGESS. She's right, Em. What would this world be like if we were all alike? [*Regards the mistletoe, remains on chair.*] —There, I think it looks very nice. I remember when I was a girl—years ago--it was 1915—

no, it was 1916—well, believe me, *we* didn't sniff at mistletoe in those days.

[*Outside door slams off Right.* JULIE *exits to dining room.*]

EMILY. [*Pensively.*] I bet it was wonderful in nineteen hundred and sixteen.

[JANET *bursts in from hall, just missing* MRS. BURGESS, *who is still on chair.* JANET *is lively and bright—twelve years old and a delightful mixture of child and adult without a trace of hateful precociousness. Still youngishly chubby. She wears a snow suit and her cheeks are vivid with cold.*]

JANET. Is Daddy home yet?

MRS. BURGESS. Janet, you almost upset me. I don't know what'd happen to your Christmas if—[*She steps from chair.*] anything'd happen to me, do *you?* I might not be here many more Christmases, anyway.

EMILY. Oh, Mother, don't talk like that!

MRS. BURGESS. [*Picks up chair.*] Well, I'm not as young as I once was, you know.

JANET. [*Patiently—as she follows* MRS. BURGESS *Left.*] Mother, is Daddy home yet?

MRS. BURGESS. Not yet, Janet.

EMILY. [*Going Right—brow furrowed.*] You make me feel so bad when you talk like that, Mother.

JANET. [*Bounding Right to* EMILY *after a second's disappointment at not finding her father there.*] Did he call yet, Em? Has Alec called yet—from Salem, Massachusetts?

EMILY. Salem! It's not Salem—it's Gloucester!

JANET. Salem sounds more historical.

EMILY. Listen to her, Mother! Probably the whole town knows it now!

JANET. Did he call?

MRS. BURGESS. [*Opening boxes up Left Center.*] You let your sister alone, Janet.

JANET. It's snowing. [*Goes to* MRS. BURGESS.] Did you know it? It's going to snow for tomorrow and Willow Pond's wonderful—all iced over. [*Begins to look through packages and pick up cards with interest.*]

EMILY. [*Goes to box near Center, gets artificial poinsettias from it.*] How's the hill, Janet?

JANET. Just right.—You want to go sledding, Em?

EMILY. [*From great heights.*] No, dear.

JANET. I remember when you used to go. You weren't bad either—I mean for a stay-at-home girl.

MRS. BURGESS. I wonder why everything gets so dusty in just one year in the attic. Whew! [*Blows dust from red paper bell she unfolds after taking it from box.*]

EMILY. [*Hanging poinsettias in window. She is Right of tree.*] I *love* Christmas!

JANET. *You* love it! [*To* MRS. BURGESS.] Has Grandpa Burgess sent anything yet?

MRS. BURGESS. Now, Janet, you know he will, so don't worry.

JANET. I know, but he always sends money, doesn't he? And I need mine as soon as it comes—before the stores close.

MRS. BURGESS. He might not send money this year.

JANET. [*Worried.*] But he always has, hasn't he? [*Goes to* EMILY.] Hasn't he, Em?

EMILY. As long as I can remember.

JANET. [*Back to* MRS. BURGESS.] There!

MRS. BURGESS. I don't think we should open anything until tomorrow.

JANET. [*Childish desperation.*] Just Grandpa's. Just his—because I need it—tonight. Please—not anything else.

MRS. BURGESS. We'll see.—Oh, what a jumble things get into!

JANET. [*Again goes to* EMILY *at window.*] Em ——

EMILY. Yes, Janet?

JANET. You'll never guess what I've got for you—you couldn't!

EMILY. No. And I'm not going to try either.

JANET. Never in a million years.

EMILY. Now, Janet, I'm not going to start that this year. I remember last year—how you made us all guess until you knew what was in every package before Christmas morning.

JANET. And Johnny thought he had a pair of slippers. I guess I fooled Johnny all right. [*Her mood changes—her voice catches.*] —Oh, Mother ——

MRS. BURGESS. Yes, Janet?—Why don't you go out now and ——

JANET. I just thought. Did you get a letter from Johnny?

MRS. BURGESS. [*Pausing—saddened.*] Yes, dear. Your brother won't be here.

EMILY. Is that definite, Mother?

JANET. Is it?

MRS. BURGESS. I'm afraid so.

JANET. [*Goes Left to sit on sofa.*] Gee. This'll be the first time, won't it? The first time that we won't all be together.

MRS. BURGESS. Yes. But his job in Chicago is important, naturally—and he just can't make it, dear, that's all.

JANET. He ought to quit! *I'd* quit!

MRS. BURGESS. [*Back to work.*] No. [*Shaking her thoughts away.*] Well, I've got a lot to do yet.

JANET. Johnny ought to quit. I wish I was in Chicago. I'd tell his boss a thing or two.

EMILY. [*Goes to sit in Right Center chair.*] It won't seem the same, will it?

JANET. He'll be so lonely there—in Chicago. I *hate* Chicago!

JULIE. [*Enters from dining room, carrying skates.*] Well, all I hope is—somebody gives me another pair of skates this year. These relics are terrible. [*Pauses Center.*]

EMILY. Oh, Julie, you're past the skate age.

JANET. [*Laughing.*] You mean the ice age. B. C.—the *ice* age!

JULIE. What would you have me get, sister?—A new formal? A book of poetry by Mr. Henry Wadsworth Longfellow?

EMILY. But skates—at sixteen!

JULIE. I'll stick to skates. You can have the poetry and the men. [*Half-heartedly and in haste.*] —Want me to help, Mother?

MRS. BURGESS. You go on—but be careful. We don't want any broken bones around here for Christmas.

JULIE. [*Relieved.*] Both my arms have already been broken, haven't they? Lightning never strikes twice in the same place. [*Starts Right—pauses.*] —Any more packages arrive?

MRS. BURGESS. A big one from your Aunt Anna, but don't start snooping.

JULIE. [*Starts to hall.*] Well, I've certainly hinted enough. If I don't get skates, it won't be my fault. [JANET *crosses to boxes on up Right table.* JULIE—*as she passes* EMILY:] When he calls, Em, give him my love.

EMILY. I will. You'll probably be waiting for some boy to call yourself, next year, then you'll understand.

JULIE. Catch me. [*Goes out in hall—the outside door slams.*]

MRS. BURGESS. Janet, don't pick at the wrappings. They always look like a lot of mice have been nibbling at them by Christmas morning. Don't you want any surprises?

JANET. I always have plenty of surprises anyway.—Did Daddy have to go out in the country?

MRS. BURGESS. He got a call from the Forrest family out on the Millersville Road.

JANET. I feel sorry for doctors. I always have wondered why Daddy wanted to be a doctor.

MRS. BURGESS. Now don't you worry your head about such things, dear.

JANET. I think I'll get my sled! [*Starts Left—pauses.*] I only wish Johnny was here to go with me. [*Goes into dining room.*]

[*Pause.* MRS. BURGESS *carries small box of ornaments and goes to sit on sofa, busy opening box—looks up.*]

MRS. BURGESS This young man who's calling, Emily— what's he like?

EMILY. He's awfully nice, Mother. You'll like him.

MRS. BURGESS. Too bad he couldn't come and spend Christmas with us.

EMILY. Oh, but he couldn't. His family always has Christmas together.

MRS. BURGESS. Yes. All over the country, I guess. It's one time of year that means a lot to a family. Makes them feel they're all one.—Only I get so tired every year I don't enjoy it the way I used to.

EMILY. [*Rises.*] Mother, you love it. All of it. The fuss and tiredness and the shopping and all of it.

MRS. BURGESS. Love it? Hum. Some day I just hope you get as tired as I do, Emily, then you'll understand.

EMILY. [*She crosses to sofa, sits, lays her head against her mother's.*] Mother ——

MRS. BURGESS. Yes—well, I guess everyone appreciates it, even if they don't say so very often.—Is it snowing hard?

EMILY. Umhum.

MRS. BURGESS. Those candles look nice, don't they?

EMILY. They look fine.

MRS. BURGESS. I only wish we had a real set of hurricane lamps. I saw some yesterday when I was downtown, but ——

EMILY. Why didn't you get them? Mother, you never get things for yourself and you should.

MRS. BURGESS. Well, maybe next year we can have crystal hurricane lamps and not just candles.

EMILY. [*Rising.*] You've been saying that for years and years. [*Goes to table up Right.*]

MRS. BURGESS. M-m-m. You know, Louise Walker who married last June is living in San Francisco now, with her husband. I saw Mrs. Walker at church last Sunday and she seemed awfully unhappy—because Louise won't be able to get home for Christmas this year.

EMILY. Louise wrote me once last July, just after she was married. She seemed terribly happy. [*Goes aimlessly to Right table.*]

MRS. BURGESS. Yes, I guess she is. Nice young man she married.

EMILY. Funny how things go, isn't it?—I mean, everything sort of shifting and changing.

MRS. BURGESS. Only natural, I guess.

EMILY. I remember Louise at the Christmas Dance last year—she was so pretty and all the boys were jealous of the fellow she married.

MRS. BURGESS. Seems just like yesterday Louise was tearing in here with snow all over her. And that Fourth of July when she burnt her hand—remember?

EMILY. [*Makes neat stacks of the opened cards on table.*] She used to play baseball like a professional pitcher.

MRS. BURGESS. Mrs. Walker said her husband just couldn't see his way clear to make the long trip. And Louise wanted to be here so bad.

EMILY. Time goes fast sometimes, doesn't it, Mother?

MRS. BURGESS. Seems to.

EMILY. It's really—terrifying—when you think of it— Louise now ——

MRS. BURGESS. Oh, she'll have her own family soon, I guess. Then it'll all seem different. She'll get used to it— I did.

EMILY. You?

MRS. BURGESS. Me. Oh, yes.—You will too.

EMILY. Oh, Mother—no!

MRS. BURGESS. Oh, yes, you will. That's just the way things go—and it's all right, too, I guess, but it makes you sad when you think of it. I hope Louise is happy.

EMILY. I'll always be here—for Christmas. **Always.**

[*Outside door closes.*]

MRS. BURGESS. Time goes on, Emily.—There's your father!

[DOCTOR TOM BURGESS *enters at hall. He is not quite fifty, a large man with sensitive eyes set like dark jewels in a wide weathered face. His hands are long and strong. He has a human air of understanding and sympathy which makes him a doctor of quality. He wears his clothes with all the easy carelessness of a boy—and in fact reminds you of a boy from time to time.*]

DOCTOR TOM. Back safe and sound, Margaret, so stop worrying.

MRS. BURGESS. I wasn't worrying, Tom. I knew you'd be all right.

DOCTOR TOM. So you convinced one of our daughters she should help you, eh? [*He is removing his coat, muffler, and hat.*]

EMILY. Dad, that's not fair.

MRS. BURGESS. Don't tease, Tom. Emily and I were having a talk.

DOCTOR TOM. [*Goes into hall to hang hat and coat—raises voice slightly.*] Snowing out. The limbs of the trees are all wrapped in ice. Going to be a real old-fashioned Christmas.

MRS. BURGESS. How are the roads?

DOCTOR TOM. [*Comes into room, goes to Right Center chair.*] Dangerous. Slick and mean. But you know my driving.

MRS. BURGESS. Who was sick at the Forrests'?

DOCTOR TOM. [*Serious.*] Mrs. Forrest.

MRS. BURGESS. Bad?

DOCTOR TOM. [*Pipe in hand.*] Oh, she'll recover.

MRS. BURGESS. That's good.

DOCTOR TOM. [*He is thoughtful.*] Yes, she'll recover.

EMILY. [*Turning.*] What's the matter, Dad?

DOCTOR TOM. Nothing, Em. Why?

EMILY. The way you sound.

MRS. BURGESS. What is it, Tom?

DOCTOR TOM. I suppose it should make me feel powerful and elated to say she'll recover but it doesn't.

MRS. BURGESS. It always has. I guess I married a pretty good doctor.

DOCTOR TOM. You know what my doctoring consisted of today?—Chopping wood.

MRS. BURGESS. Chopping ——? [*Rises—crosses to him.*] Oh, Tom, your hands. [*Takes his hands. They are red and swollen.*]

DOCTOR TOM. Look out, there! They're sore. I guess I'm not the man I once was.

MRS. BURGESS. Tom, you shouldn't do things like that.

DOCTOR TOM. Well, they were cold and they needed wood. The young ones are all too young, and without heat that woman would have died in the next couple of days.

EMILY. What a terrible Christmas they ——

MRS. BURGESS. You must be dead.

DOCTOR TOM. Well, I'm hungry.

MRS. BURGESS. [*Starts to dining room. Pauses up of sofa Left.*] What about some coffee? How would some mince pie ——

[JANET *dashes in from the hall, covered with snow.*]

JANET. Any word from Grandpa Burgess?

MRS. BURGESS. Not yet, Janet. Come along, Tom.

DOCTOR TOM. [*Rises.*] Janet, I saw you sledding in the street as I came by.

JANET. [*At Center.*] Me?

DOCTOR TOM. [*Softly, gently, firmly.*] Yes—you. And if you can't stick to the hill with your sled, we'll have to find other uses for the wood in it. It burns very well, do you know that?

JANET. I only went in the street once.

DOCTOR TOM. [*Wisely skeptical.*] M-m-m. The time I was driving by. That old car of ours won't stop on ice, you know. Have I got your promise, Janet?

JANET. I promise. [*Sees* DOCTOR TOM's *hands.*] —Daddy, your hands! What's happened? They're all swollen!

DOCTOR TOM. [*Running his hand through her hair, taking her hat.*] Well, it was this way: you know that big oak by the Millersville Bridge ——

JANET. [*Taken in.*] Yes.

DOCTOR TOM. Well, there it was across the road ——

MRS. BURGESS. Tom ——

JANET. You mean the wind blew that big old oak down?

DOCTOR TOM. So there was only one thing to do ——

JANET. I always liked that tree. It was sort of twisted and funny.

DOCTOR TOM. I had to get out of the car right there on the spot and lift it off the road.

JANET. Lift it? [*Realizing.*] Aw, how old do you think I am?

[*Everyone laughs.*]

DOCTOR TOM. About eighty—*are* you that old, Janet?

JANET. Well, I'm old enough to know a lot of things no one else knows.

DOCTOR TOM. [*Going Left to dining room.*] You come on out and tell me.

JANET. About Julie.

MRS. BURGESS. [*Immediately worried. Turning in doorway.*] Julie!—Has she fallen?

JANET. [*Breaks into laughter.*] *Fallen!* That's good! [*Laughs.*] Yes, she's fallen all right, but not the way you mean. [*Laughs.*]

EMILY. What do you mean, Janet?

JANET. I mean a lot. She's skating with that new boy that moved into the Richards' old house—his name's Ralph something-or-other.

EMILY. Julie's skating with a *boy?*

DOCTOR TOM. Well, about time!

MRS. BURGESS. Now that's no way to talk. Let Julie do as she likes.

JANET. Did I make her blush! I didn't know Julie was the kind who blushed.

EMILY. And just ten minutes ago she was making fun of me!

MRS. BURGESS. You leave her alone, Janet. You'll skate with a boy yourself some day and you won't want any smaller sister making jibes.

JANET. I don't have any smaller sister—and I already skate with boys.

DOCTOR TOM. You do? You make me jealous, Janet.

JANET. Daddy, I'm twelve. Don't you know that? How old do you really think I am?

DOCTOR TOM. [*Laughing.*] Miss Methuselah!

JANET. [*Goes down to her father.*] You know what I wish ——

MRS. BURGESS. I thought you were hungry, Tom.

DOCTOR TOM. Just a moment, dear.—What do you wish, Janet?

JANET. I wish I could just *stay* twelve. I really do. And I wish Johnny would come home and we'd all stay just the way we are—forever.—And something else ——

DOCTOR TOM. It's already a big order, Janet.

JANET. I wish Grandpa Williams was still with us. [DOC-

TOR TOM *flashes a look at* MRS. BURGESS *who looks away.*]
I wouldn't even mind his teasing and his jokes if only he
was still—with us.

DOCTOR TOM. Well, I don't think Grandpa Williams would
want us to grieve for him on Christmas Eve. [*Puts arm
around* MRS. BURGESS.] I think he'd want us to have a
good time—the way he always did. Don't you, Margaret?

MRS. BURGESS. I suppose so. Yes, I suppose that's just
what he would want.—But when I think of just last year
he was here—and always laughing—and crazy as a child
about the gifts—and hanging the lights on the tree ——
[*She turns away.*]

JANET. Oh, Mother, I didn't mean to make you cry.

MRS. BURGESS. I know. I'm foolish.

JANET. [*Going to sofa.*] It's just that I loved him so much
—and I never knew how much all the time he was with
us—and now —— [JANET *sinks to sofa. A moment's
pause.*]

DOCTOR TOM. Well, I don't mind telling you what I wish—
I wish Johnny was here, up to his old tricks—and singing
off-tune in the bathtub and stealing my ties—and bumping
in a fender now and then. There—that's what the old man
wishes!

EMILY. My, it's getting late, isn't it?

JANET. Oh, Alec'll call.

EMILY. I didn't mean *that!*

JANET. Isn't that a funny name—Alec! Grandpa'd laugh
at that name!

MRS. BURGESS. Father laughed at *everything.*

DOCTOR TOM. Well, it'd be great to hear Johnny come whistling in that front door, but what is to be, you know ——

JANET. *Auld Lang Syne*—that's what he'd be whistling! [*Sings.*] "Should old acquaintance be forgot ——" He always whistled that.

DOCTOR TOM. All we can hope is that he has a good Christmas in Chicago. Come on, Marge—I'm getting hungrier by the second.

[MRS. BURGESS *and* DOCTOR TOM *go into dining room.* EMILY *runs her hand over the phone.*]

EMILY. My, it's getting late. [*Goes to sit by* JANET *on sofa.*] It's getting dark, isn't it?

JANET. [*Moves close to* EMILY.] It'll soon be Christmas. I hope there are a lot of stars—millions of stars.

EMILY. I wish he'd call if he's going to. Does he think I haven't anything else to do all Christmas Eve?

JANET. Can I turn on the tree now?

EMILY. It's still pretty early. It'd be nice, but I think you better wait.

JANET. Emily, you'd never guess in a trillion years what I've got for you.

EMILY. Now don't start that again, silly. I won't try.

JANET. All right.—What time do the stores close, Em?

EMILY. They stay open late tonight, I think.

JANET. If Grandpa's gift doesn't come, I won't be able ——

EMILY. —To what?

JANET. Oh, never mind. Don't you wish you knew?

[JULIE *enters from hall—slightly ill at ease.*]

EMILY. Hello, Julie.

[RALPH WEATHERLY *follows her in.* RALPH *is seventeen, not particularly handsome, but his wide, pleasant smile and slight embarrassed uneasiness are engaging. He carries his skates.*]

JULIE. Hello, Em. And Janet.

JANET. [*To* RALPH.] Say, you're a real skater! [*Rises and crosses to Right Center chair.*]

RALPH. Why, thanks.

JANET. I saw you skating on the pond with Julie—around the edges—very slow.

JULIE. [*At Center.*] Ralph, I'd like for you to know my sisters. This is Emily and this is Janet—Ralph Weatherly.

JANET. Weatherly? I never heard a name like that before.

RALPH. [*Smiling nervously.*] Well, neither did I.—How do you do?

EMILY. How do you do, Mr. Weatherly?

JANET. " Mister?"

JULIE. Ralph is new to town.

RALPH. We just moved in two weeks ago.

JANET. I saw you. You've got a swell pair of skis. I saw them when you moved in.

JULIE. [*Scandalized.*] Janet ——

RALPH. Well—thanks.

JANET. Julie can ski like the wind.

RALPH. I'm glad to hear that.

JANET. —And you should see Johnny swoop down Spring Hill. He looks like a Viking.

JULIE. You'd like Johnny, Ralph. He's our brother.

EMILY. Janet, let's you and I go up and get dressed for supper.

JANET. [*Goes to Right—speaks nervously.*] You know, Ralph, I'm glad to see Julie going out with boys ——

JULIE. Janet Burgess!

JANET. Just this evening I said ——

EMILY. [*Quickly.*] Janet, come on now, we're going upstairs and dress for supper. You look like a ragamuffin.

JANET. —So it's good to see you, Ralph. I hope I see you a lot.

EMILY. [*Propelling* JANET *forcibly toward the hall.*] Here we go.—Julie, if the phone rings, be sure to call me. I'm pleased to have met you, Mr. Weatherly.

[JANET *and* EMILY *go into hall.*]

RALPH. Thanks.—So am I.

[*Pause.*]

JULIE. Really, she's awfully little.

RALPH. I think she's great. I wish I had a kid sister. [*He places skates on floor near table up Right.*]

JULIE. But she says such funny things—sometimes.

RALPH. She didn't say anything funny that I heard. She sounded pretty sensible. I hope she does see me a lot—because I'm going to be around a lot. [JULIE *looks at him.*] That is, if it's all right with you, Julie.

JULIE. [*Softly.*] It's all right with me, I think, Ralph.

RALPH. Because I've had a great time this afternoon, Julie. Have you?

JULIE. I've had a wonderful time. I didn't realize how wonderful a time you could have—just skating.

RALPH. Neither did I.

JULIE. —And I've skated on Willow Pond all my life.

RALPH. Have you? I wish I'd lived here in town longer. I wish I'd been born here, I mean.

JULIE. So do I, Ralph.

RALPH. Funny, isn't it—how we've just known each other for a few hours and yet I feel like I've known you a long time?

JULIE. Oh, we've known each other longer than that. We were introduced at school last week, don't you remember?

RALPH. Sure, I remember. But we didn't really know each other. I just thought you were another girl then.

JULIE. And I don't think I liked you very much. [*Goes to sit on sofa.*]

RALPH. Didn't you? I was nervous, I guess. I get nervous pretty easy.

JULIE. Anyway, you seemed a lot different today.

RALPH. [Sits beside her.] Do you know something?

JULIE. What?

RALPH. We're talking more now than we talked all afternoon.

JULIE. That's right, isn't it?

RALPH. But it was fun—skating around not talking.

JULIE. The snow felt like silk blowing against your face.

RALPH. I'm going to like this town.

JULIE. I hope so. I've always liked it. Do you know—I've always been more like a boy than a girl—but I've had loads of fun all my life—except when my Grandpa Williams died last July. That just about broke this family up for weeks.

RALPH. I'm sorry.

JULIE. You see, he lived here. You'll think it funny, but I was thinking about him some of the time when we were skating. I don't know why.

RALPH. Maybe because you liked him so much.

JULIE. Maybe.—I was wondering whether he was like you when he was young. He might have been.

RALPH. Makes you feel funny, doesn't it?—Thinking about him when he was young. I wonder what it was like back then.

JULIE. I wouldn't have liked it, the way some people would. Em would probably like it all right, but I'm too much of a tomboy. I guess I'd've been a real misfit in those days.

RALPH. I wouldn't've thought so, though.

JULIE. Really, Ralph?

RALPH. You know I wouldn't've. Gosh, Julie, I think I'd've met you any time we'd both happen to be living.

JULIE. Do you think that too?

RALPH. Do you?

JULIE. I think that, yes.

RALPH. Julie ——

JULIE. Yes ——

RALPH. Would you mind if I—if I—kissed you, Julie?

JULIE. Kiss me?

RALPH. It's all right if you don't want me to ——

JULIE. Oh, it's not that. It's not that. I just—it's just I never kissed a boy before ——

RALPH. No?

JULIE. No.

RALPH. —Then maybe ——

JULIE. I didn't mean I wouldn't.—I don't think I'd mind at all, Ralph.—You.

RALPH. Julie ——

JULIE. Wait! I just thought. [*Rises and crosses to hall entrance.*] The mistletoe.

RALPH. [*Rising, follows her.*] Oh.—You know, you're so different, Julie.

JULIE. All right now, Ralph.

[*He kisses her—first on the forehead, then on the lips lightly—stands back.*]

RALPH. [*Hushed.*] Julie Burgess.

JULIE. [*Just as hushed.*] Ralph Weatherly.

RALPH. Will I see you tomorrow, Julie?

JULIE. I wish you would.

RALPH. Before noon? [*He still holds her hand.*]

JULIE. Right after church.

RALPH. Will your mother care?

JULIE. She won't mind. At least I don't *think* she'll mind.

RALPH. Maybe I should go now.

JULIE. Maybe you should.

RALPH. But it won't be long until tomorrow. I know—I'll call you on the telephone tonight—to wish you Merry Christmas. Will you be up?

JULIE. We're always up till very late on Christmas Eve.

DOCTOR TOM. [*Enters from dining room.*] Oh, pardon me, Julie.

[RALPH *quickly relinquishes* JULIE's *hand.*]

JULIE. Don't go, Dad. I'd like to have you meet Ralph Weatherly.—This is my father.

RALPH. How do you do, sir?

DOCTOR TOM. I'm fine, thank you.—Say, I don't believe I know you, do I?

RALPH. I just moved to town, sir.

DOCTOR TOM. Oh, yes. Weatherly. Oh, yes.

RALPH. I must be going now. It's about time for supper and the family likes to eat early on Christmas Eve.

DOCTOR TOM. I see.

RALPH. [*Getting skates from floor.*] We've had a fine skate, Julie and I.

DOCTOR TOM. I don't doubt it. You'll have to come around again sometime, Ralph.

RALPH. Thanks.

JULIE. He'll be over in the morning, Dad.

DOCTOR TOM. Good.

RALPH. Good night, sir.—Good night, Julie.

JULIE. Good night, Ralph—and don't forget. [*As they go into hall.*]

RALPH. I won't. Just before twelve.

JULIE. I'll be waiting. [DOCTOR TOM *sits in chair Right Center.* JULIE *returns.* DOCTOR TOM *has a worried expression.*] Well, Dad ——

DOCTOR TOM. Well, what?

JULIE. Do you like him?

DOCTOR TOM. Oh, you mean the boy. Yes, I like him. [*Smiles.*] We didn't get very well acquainted, you know.

JULIE. No—but you *do* like him, don't you?

DOCTOR TOM. Do you?

JULIE. Very much. Very much.

DOCTOR TOM. Then so do I.

JULIE. [*Notices his preoccupation.*] What is it, Daddy? You look so sad tonight.

DOCTOR TOM. Do I?

JULIE. You mustn't be sad tonight, Daddy. Not tonight —of all nights. This is one of the most wonderful nights there ever was. [*Goes into hall.*]

[DOCTOR TOM *smiles after her. The worried expression returns immediately and his head sinks to his hands. Pause Then* EMILY *enters from the hall. She goes behind him and places her hand on his shoulder quietly.*]

EMILY. You're worried about the Forrest family, aren't you, Dad?

DOCTOR TOM. [*Not lifting his head.*] Yes, Emily.

EMILY. I have too. Even though I was all wrapped up in my own troubles, I have too—along the edges of my mind.

DOCTOR TOM. It won't be a very nice Christmas for them, you know—with the mother in bed and only a fire. They don't have one toy and very little food. They wouldn't call me, you know—too proud, because they can't pay the bill they owe me.

EMILY. Foolish.

DOCTOR TOM. Yes, foolish. But you can't tell them that.

EMILY. No, I suppose not.—Dad—I have a little money —oh, not very much, but a little—and if you had a little too ——

DOCTOR TOM. That's what worries me. After all this Christmas spending, I'm always about as poor as a church mouse.

[JANET *and* JULIE *enter hand in hand.*]

EMILY. Well, Mother might have some too, mightn't she? —And Julie. I don't think Janet has any.

JANET. Has any what?

EMILY. Any money.

JANET. [*Goes Center.*] I have a little—for something very, very *special!*

JULIE. [*Now near* JANET.] What do you want money for, Em?

EMILY. For the Forrests. They live out on the Millersville Road and they haven't even any coal—or anything else, I guess.

JULIE. Oh ——

JANET. And no Christmas tree?

DOCTOR TOM. I'm afraid not, Janet.

JANET. That's *awful!*

EMILY. Here's mine—three dollars. [*Places it on arm of Right Center chair.*]

JULIE. [*Reaching in pocket.*] Two is all I have, Dad.

DOCTOR TOM. Now you listen to me, all of you kids. I

haven't asked you for anything. I haven't even brought it up for that very reason ——

JULIE. We know that ——

DOCTOR TOM. And if you don't want to do it, just say so.

EMILY. Dad, it's Christmas.

[JULIE *places her money with* EMILY'S. MRS. BURGESS *enters from dining room. Her eyes are red with crying.*]

DOCTOR TOM. [*Going Left to her.*] Margaret ——

MRS. BURGESS. Now don't fuss over me.

JULIE. You've been crying.

MRS. BURGESS. And what if I have, young lady? I've seen you cry before.

JULIE. But why ——?

[MRS. BURGESS *sits on sofa.*]

DOCTOR TOM. Now, Julie, that's enough. We all miss your brother and your grandfather this Christmas and we'll all probably show it a little, won't we? Sit down now and rest, Margaret —— [*Goes to Christmas tree.*] I'll turn on a few lights.

EMILY. How much do you have, Dad?

[EMILY *and* JULIE *go to* MRS. BURGESS *and sit on sofa, leaning against her.* JANET *remains up Center, fingering the tree—lost in thought—quite alone. The tree lights come on.*]

JULIE. Oh! Isn't it beautiful?

MRS. BURGESS. Yes, isn't it?

DOCTOR TOM. [*At Center pulls a five dollar bill out of his pocket.*] Ten dollars, all told. We can do a lot with that.

[*Puts it on arm of chair.*]

MRS. BURGESS. For the Forrests?

DOCTOR TOM. Yes, dear.

MRS. BURGESS. The most I could raise would be about three more. I'll get it before you go.

[*There is a knock at the door.* JANET *goes into hall.*]

DOCTOR TOM. [*Goes up of sofa—places hand on* MRS. BURGESS'S *shoulder.*] Now don't grieve today, Margaret. We'll all pile in the car later and go down to buy some clothes and some food for the Forrests.

EMILY. I want to go out with you when you go.

JULIE. I do too.—But what about some toys? Wouldn't they like toys?

DOCTOR TOM. I think we'd better spend what we have on food and clothes.

JULIE. Still, it won't be Christmas without any toys.

JANET. [*Returning with a special delivery envelope.*] It's from Grandpa Burgess. [*Her shoulders droop and she is not excited.*]

MRS. BURGESS. [*To* JANET.] Well, you don't seem very excited about it now that it's here, Janet. [*To* DOCTOR TOM.] Should we open it tonight, Tom?

DOCTOR TOM. [*Goes Center to take envelope.*] I can't see why not.

JANET. Oh, you've *got* to! I've got to get something.

MRS. BURGESS. It can't be that important.

[DOCTOR TOM *goes Right.*]

EMILY. [*Rises.*] Oh, say, I've got an idea. Why don't we take Grandfather's money and buy toys for the Forrests? We could be real Santa Claus for them, then.

JULIE. Sure!

JANET. [*Deflated.*] Oh, no! [ALL *turn to her. She looks at them.*] I mean—well, I've really got other plans for that money, *really*. I've been planning on something for weeks and saving—even months. That's why I couldn't give anything just now.

DOCTOR TOM. Well, then, the rest of us can give ours and Janet can do what she wants with hers. It's a good idea, Emily. I'm just a little proud of my family, aren't you, Mother?

MRS. BURGESS. I'm very proud of all of them. It feels more like Christmas already.

JANET. But listen—I don't want you to think I'm selfish. Honest—it's not that.

DOCTOR TOM. Janet, no one has suggested that you are. We'll have plenty this way.

JANET. But ——

[*There is the sound of a whistle.*]

DOCTOR TOM. Shh.

[*Pause. They are all frozen. A long moment. The tune is clear now: " Auld Lang Syne."*]

EMILY. Johnny ——!!

JULIE. Johnny ——!!

[*Sound of a door opening.*]

DOCTOR TOM. I think you're right, children.

JOHNNY'S VOICE. [*Singing now—off.*] " We'll take a cup o' kindness yet, For auld lang syne." [*Calls.*] Hey, look what Santa Claus brought.

[DOCTOR TOM *crosses to* MRS. BURGESS *and gives her his handkerchief. She hasn't moved but her eyes are filling with tears.* JANET *goes up Left almost into corner.*]

DOCTOR TOM. Here you are, Mother—clean.

[JOHNNY *enters from hall. He is a boyish twenty-one, sandy-haired, slim, with direct eyes—and a gay excited manner at the moment, his arms filled with packages.*]

JOHNNY. Merry Christmas!

JULIE. [*Going to him.*] Merry Christmas, Johnny! Merry Christmas!

DOCTOR TOM. Hello, son. [*Shakes hands with* JOHNNY.]

EMILY. Here's Mother, Johnny.

JOHNNY. [*Goes down Center.*] Merry Christmas, Mother!

MRS. BURGESS. [*Almost a reprimand—but happy.*] Johnny, why didn't you write?

JOHNNY. I couldn't. I just got away at the last minute and hopped the train as it was pulling out—nearly killed myself getting on.

MRS. BURGESS. [*Rising to embrace him.*] You be careful of those trains. You be careful.

[*After the embrace, the* OTHERS *crowd around him,* JULIE *and* EMILY *kissing him.* JANET *remains up Left.* JOHNNY *removes coat, tossing it across sofa.*]

JULIE. Why not telegraph, Johnny?

JOHNNY. The surprise is better.

EMILY. It's all we needed, Johnny. I was never so glad to see you before in my whole life.

DOCTOR TOM. Welcome home, son.

JOHNNY. Gosh, Dad, I was worried—I didn't think I'd make it in time for Christmas Eve.—Say, haven't I got another sister? [*Sees* JANET.] What's the matter with my wild Janet? [*Goes to her.*] Hello, you.

JANET. [*Her lips trembling.*] Hello, Johnny.

JOHNNY. Why, what is all this?

JANET. [*Going into his arms.*] Oh, Johnny!

[MRS. BURGESS *sits in chair Right Center.* DOCTOR TOM *goes Right.* JULIE *is up Left with* JOHNNY *and* JANET. *Telephone rings. Pause. They turn to* EMILY. *She goes to phone.*]

EMILY. Hello, Burgess residence.—Yes.—This is Miss Emily Burgess speaking ——

JANET. [*To* JOHNNY.] It's her fellow. He's calling all the way from Massachusetts.

[*During the following phone conversation,* JOHNNY *and* JANET *converse in whispers. The* OTHERS *whisper and exchange glances as they are trying not to listen to* EMILY.]

EMILY. Hello. [*Her face lights up. She shoots a self-con-scious glance at the family.*]—Oh, hello, Alec. Yes, it's snowing here, too.—Yes.—And my brother Johnny got home from Chicago after all.—What? [*Her voice changes to a whisper.*] What? [*Pause.*] Yes, yes, I'm still here, Alec.—No, I didn't faint.—Why, I don't know, Alec—it isn't fair—like this. [MRS. BURGESS *silently reaches out to* DOCTOR TOM *who takes her hand.*] I'll tell you when I see you at school. [*Laughs a little unnaturally.*] That's not long, Alec—just after New Year's.—Yes.—And Merry Christmas to you—and all of them! Tomorrow? Well, you can call—but I won't give you any answer—until after New Year's.—But please call!—Good-bye, Alec.

[*She hangs up gently and turns slowly.* MRS. BURGESS *is watching her.* JULIE *has turned and has heard.*]

JULIE. [*Not quite knowing what to say.*] Well, I guess I'd better put on a coat if we're going out.

EMILY. [*Uncertainly, slowly.*] He said to tell everyone Merry Christmas.

MRS. BURGESS. Yes, Emily?

EMILY. And—he—also asked me to—to—marry him in the Spring—and I said—I said—I'd think it over. [*She goes into hall quickly.*]

[*Long pause.* MRS. BURGESS *looks to* DOCTOR TOM.]

MRS. BURGESS. She's just a child—Emily.

JOHNNY. Married? Emily?

DOCTOR TOM. [*Slowly.*] Well, well, well.

MRS. BURGESS. [*Rising.*] Come along, Janet—we'll put on some coats and mufflers.

DOCTOR TOM. [*Goes Center.*] Johnny, we're driving out into the country soon. Like to come along?

JOHNNY. Sure.

MRS. BURGESS. [*Goes to hall entrance, waits.*] Come on now, Janet.

DOCTOR TOM. Emily married. Well, it hardly seems possible, that's all.—Coming, Janet?

JANET. All right.

DOCTOR TOM. [*Separates envelopes and takes money from arm of chair and jams it into a pocket.*] Here's your envelope from Grandpa, Janet.

JANET. Thank you. [*She takes it and in a burst of crying brushes past them and into the hall.*]

JOHNNY. What does all that mean?

DOCTOR TOM. Sh-h, Johnny. [*Holds up his hand.*] It'll all work itself out.

MRS. BURGESS. Emily married and Father gone. [*Shakes her head and goes into hall.* DOCTOR TOM *follows.*]

JULIE. [*Enters, getting into her coat.*] Johnny ——

JOHNNY. Hello, Julie. You look a lot older, do you know that?

JULIE. Maybe I am, Johnny.—There's someone I want you to meet, Johnny. You'll like him.

JOHNNY. [*He picks up coat and gets into it.*] A boy?

JULIE. Of course, silly.

JOHNNY. [*Smiling.*] Well, I hope he's a swell fellow, Julie. Be careful though.

JULIE. Careful? Isn't that silly?

JOHNNY. People aren't always what they seem, that's all—and it can hurt like the devil to find it out. Will you remember that?

JULIE. I don't need to, Johnny. Not with Ralph.

JOHNNY. [*Smiling.*] I hope not.

JULIE. Don't be so serious.

[JANET *enters and goes to sit silently alone in chair Right Center.* JOHNNY *watches her.*]

JOHNNY. Where are we going?

JULIE. We're going to make a real Christmas for one of Dad's patients.

[EMILY, MRS. BURGESS, *and* DOCTOR TOM *enter—putting on coats.*]

EMILY. Please do sing, Mother. I'll play.

MRS. BURGESS. But my voice has all gone—a long time ago. Don't keep urging me.

DOCTOR TOM. Johnny, you try to convince her. Remember how she used to sing the carols—every Christmas?

EMILY. I'll go play. [*Goes out again into hall.*]

JOHNNY. Why not, Mother?

[*Warn Curtain.*]

MRS. BURGESS. [*At Center.*] I've got the voice of an old crow.

[*Piano begins, "It Came Upon the Midnight Clear"—or other appropriate carol.*]

DOCTOR TOM. [*Singing.*] "It came upon a midnight clear, That glorious song of old."

[JULIE *joins him. Also* JOHNNY. JANET *sits alone staring front.*]

DOCTOR TOM, JULIE and JOHNNY.

"From angels bending near the earth
To touch their harps of gold ——"

[MRS. BURGESS *joins in in a clear fine voice. Gradually the* OTHERS *stop singing and she is singing alone.*]

MRS. BURGESS.

"Peace on earth, good will to men
From Heaven's all gracious King,
The world in solemn stillness lay
To hear the angels sing."

JANET. [*Rises and goes over to her mother—very fast.*] You can have mine too, Mother—for the Forrests. I really didn't want it for myself. [*Tearfully.*] I just wanted to get you the lamps you've been wanting, that's all—for Christmas. But we've already got so much—so *very* much —and I love it all so—take the money, Dad—and go on singing, Mother—please.

[MRS. BURGESS *bends down and hugs* JANET *to her. The* OTHERS *are grouped about.*]

JOHNNY. What lamps? Hurricane lamps? Ho-ho—Johnny beat you to it. I brought a set from Chicago!

DOCTOR TOM. [*To* MRS. BURGESS, *laughing.*] You and your lamps!

JANET. Let's sing again! Let me sing too!

[EMILY *strikes a chord: "Jingle Bells."*]

MRS. BURGESS. Let's go now!

[*They go into the hall together. First one, then another, and finally all are singing "Jingle Bells" with great good spirits as they leave and* DOCTOR TOM *turns off, first, the lights in the room, leaving only the tree lighted—then the tree lights go off—and the singing is heard off, as the Curtain falls.*]

CURTAIN

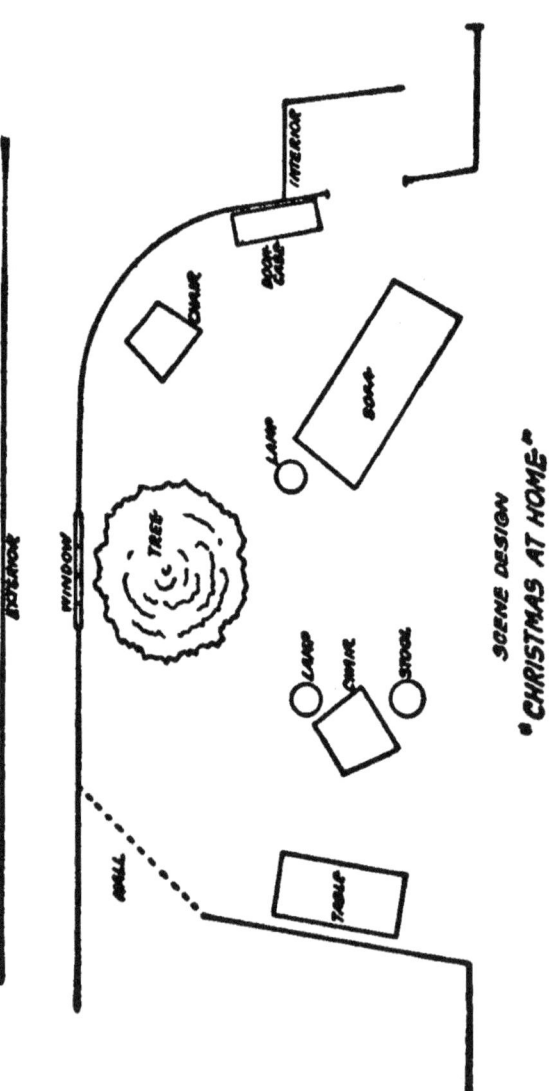

SCENE DESIGN
"CHRISTMAS AT HOME"

www.ingramcontent.com/pod-product-compliance
Lightning Source LLC
Chambersburg PA
CBHW070403120726
47909CB00008B/2968